FINAL CUT

FINAL CUT

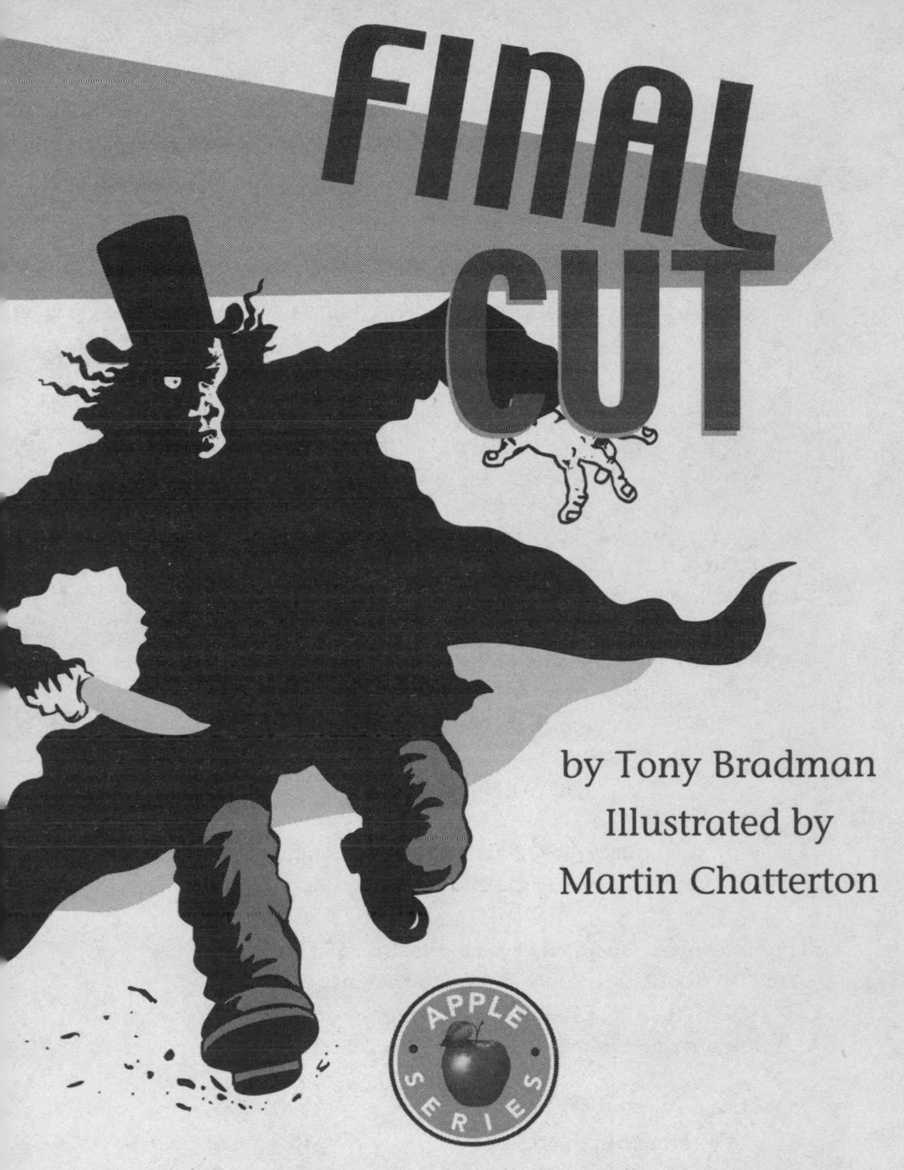

by Tony Bradman

Illustrated by

Martin Chatterton

SCHOLASTIC INC.
New York Toronto London Auckland Sydney
Mexico City New Delhi Hong Kong Buenos Aires

ISBN 0-439-79597-4

 Published by Scholastic Inc., 557 Broadway, New York, NY 10012, by arrangement with Egmont Books Limited.

12 11 10 9 8 7 6 5 4 3 2 1 6 7 8 9 10/0
Printed in the U.S.A. 40
First Scholastic printing, January 2006

CONTENTS

FINAL CUT

IN HIDING

It's the end of the school day, and Billy Gibson is hiding in the boys' room.

Billy stands in a closed stall, his back to the door, his bag clutched to his chest. He listens as the building beyond empties. Above him, gray winter light seeps in from the line of narrow windows over the sinks, but the cold air is already thickening into late-afternoon darkness. Billy shifts his feet uneasily. His mouth is dry and he can feel his heart thudding in his chest.

He wonders if it's safe yet to go outside, make a dash for home.

The school slowly grows quieter, the shouts and screams fading to distant murmurs, the thuds of heavily shod feet in the hallways becoming the tap-tapping of a single pair of shoes, silence falling at last. Billy holds his breath, waits a few more seconds . . . and the silence continues unbroken. *Time to get moving,* he thinks, breathing out, hitching his bag onto his shoulder.

He slips from the stall, heads for the door into the hallway, his own footsteps echoing. He reaches for the door handle — but the door swings open before his hand touches it and three boys stride in.

The one in the middle is blond-haired and about the same size as Billy. He has a small, narrow mouth and pointed features. The other two are big and solidly built, both with their heads shaved close to the skull, the pair almost indistinguishable from each other. Billy knows who all three of them are, and he breathes in sharply. He retreats as they advance and soon finds himself backed up against the sinks. He covers his chest with his bag, his heart whacking wildly against his ribs now. *Like a caged bird trying to escape,* Billy thinks, part of his mind oddly distant, observing.

He feels sick, his stomach twisting into a knot.

"Well, here's where you are, Billy," says the blond-haired boy, coming to a halt in front of him. "We've been looking for you everywhere, haven't we, guys?" The other two don't answer, take up positions on either side of Billy. "I was beginning to think you might be hiding from us," continues the blond-haired boy, smiling at him. "Although why would you want to do that?"

Because you're Mickey Travis, the school's top bully, thinks Billy, *and Tweedledum and Tweedledee here are your thugs, and the three of you have been bullying me for the past month.* But the thought remains unvoiced.

The bullying had started when Billy got a good grade for some English homework — a story he'd written — and the teacher had told the class. There had been a little light pushing and shoving afterward, but Billy

had ignored it, hoping that if he didn't make trouble, Mickey would lose interest and move on to somebody else. The rough stuff got heavier, though, Mickey and his pals adding slaps and kicks to another bout of jostling the next day.

Billy put up with that, too, choosing to take the path of least resistance, worried that if he didn't he'd only make Mickey angry and things would get worse. Which they did, anyway, with Mickey graduating to demanding money and getting meaner, the slaps becoming punches, the kicks a lot more painful.

So Billy had decided it was time to devise a new plan.

He'd thought about telling his teachers or his mom and dad, but quickly ruled out both options. They probably wouldn't believe him or do anything. And Billy dreaded to think what Mickey might do if he discovered he'd been ratted on. No, Billy had come to the conclusion there was only one thing to do: He would have to keep out of Mickey's way, avoid him. Hide.

But that hasn't worked, either, Billy thinks as he stands in the dank gloom of the boys' room. Mickey had probably known where he was all the time.

"Hiding? Me?" says Billy nervously. "What makes you think that?"

"Oh, I don't know," says Mickey, his smile vanishing. "I wondered if you might be trying to get out of handing over the money you owe me."

"Listen, Mickey," Billy murmurs. "Can we talk about this?"

"I don't think so, Billy," says Mickey. "Do your stuff, boys."

Mickey steps out of the way, and Billy feels his arms being grabbed, a meaty hand on his neck, his legs kicked out from underneath him. Then he's on the floor, his face pushed into the damp, gritty concrete, his nostrils filled with a smell that makes him want to throw up, a mixture of old dust and dirt laced with something acrid and foul. He wriggles, tries to get free, but he's held down, Mickey's boys grinding their knees into his back and legs.

He feels Mickey's unhurried, careful hands going through his pockets one by one. And Billy feels other things, too: a brief flash of anger at those probing, alien fingers; a sharp, sudden flare of hatred for Mickey Travis and his gang.

Mickey eventually finds what he's after, takes his fingers away. "Let him up," he says, and the other two obey.

Billy rises and brushes the dirt off his clothes, checks himself for any major damage. He seems to be mostly all right, although his cheek is hurting where it was pressed into the floor. Mickey is counting the small collection of coins he's extracted from Billy's pockets. He looks at Billy, frowns.

"Tsk, tsk, Billy," Mickey says, and sighs deeply. "This isn't

going to make me rich, is it? You'd better come up with a lot more tomorrow."

"I . . . I can't," Billy stammers. "I mean, I only get my lunch money. . . ."

Billy notices that Tweedledum has picked up his bag.

"Well, that's not my problem, is it, Billy?" says Mickey, smiling at him again. "I'm sure you'll think of something. You're a born loser, pal. It's written all over you, and you'll never, ever change. So we both know you'll always do exactly what I tell you. Just in case, though, here's a sneak preview of what will happen tomorrow — if you let me down."

Mickey nods at Tweedledum. The boy goes into a stall, dumps the contents of Billy's bag into the toilet bowl with a clatter and splash, a red pen bouncing off the rim and skittering across the floor to lie at Mickey's feet. He chucks the bag in, too, stuffs it in hard, and flushes, grinning.

Mickey picks up the pen, tucks it in Billy's pocket. "Take my advice, Billy," he says. "Be sensible . . . and go with the flow." His goons smirk, and Mickey laughs softly. "Believe me, you don't want it to be your head down there next time. So long for now, loser. Enjoy the rest of your day."

Mickey and his boys make their exit, the door swinging shut behind them, cutting off their loud, echoing laughter. Billy waits for a moment, getting his feelings — and his breathing — under control, trying to calm down. Then he goes into the stall to retrieve his bag, salvage his books. But a glance in the bowl tells him he doesn't want to touch either the bag or the books.

He'll have to come up with some excuse, he thinks, say he lost them, left his bag on the bus, take the consequences. He doesn't have any other choice.

Billy opens the door of the boys' room. He peers outside, making sure that Mickey and his thugs have really left. The school's central hallway is reassuringly empty beneath its ceiling lights, pools of brightness alternating with stripes of shadow on the polished floor that stretches ahead of him.

Billy sets off, trudges past dark, deserted classrooms.

He pushes open the doors at the end of the hall, walks out into the playground. That's empty as well, black puddles dotted across the pavement between him and the school's main gates, the sky filling with clouds. He feels the skin tightening over the bones of his face, realizes how cold it is. He buttons up his jacket, his breath a silver mist around his head. Billy pauses for a moment. He'll just have to ask his parents for his allowance early this week. But that's OK, they won't mind. Then he'll be safe, he'll be able to give Mickey more than today. But Billy doesn't feel better, and he knows why. He stands brooding, Mickey's words echoing in his mind.

"You're a born loser, pal. It's written all over you . . ."

Billy considers his appearance, wonders how it's possible to look like a loser and not realize it. He knows he's a little shy and quiet, not athletic or cool or funny like some people. But there must be something he can shine at, some way of showing Mickey he's not a loser, that there's more to him.

Billy feels the wind whip at his pant legs, a few spots of rain on his face. *It's not a bad plan,* he thinks, and starts racking his brains for some activity he could pursue. He's good at writing stories, but that's not going to impress someone like Mickey, is it? Otherwise, Billy's mind is a total blank. He sighs, sets off again, shoulders sagging as he trudges around the school building, following the path to the small back gate he always uses.

The surfaces of the puddles shiver in the wind, as if an invisible giant has passed a hand across them. Thick clouds shroud the last of the light. Beyond the fence, a streetlamp fizzes, then flickers on, and another does the same, then another. Billy's shoes tap-tap on the pavement. He turns a corner, and suddenly, the air before him shimmers for a second. Billy shakes his head . . .

And stops dead in his tracks, his mouth dropping open with surprise.

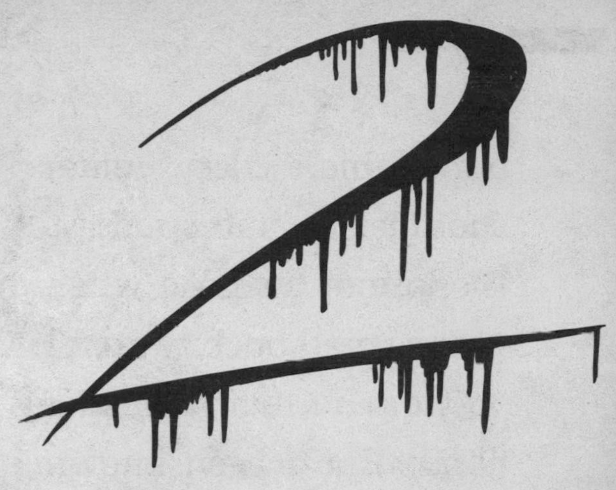

THE STRANGERS

Billy is facing the part of the playground that's completely hidden from the street, a scuffy patch of cracked asphalt that leads to the bike sheds and the small back gate. A rusty fire escape zigzags up the building's four stories where, at lunchtime, cocky older kids gather in its shadows to pose and smoke when the teachers on duty aren't looking. Other, nastier things have been known to happen there occasionally, too.

It should be empty and safe now — but it isn't. It's full of movement and machines and strangers, a bustling crowd of grown-ups under bright lights on

stands. Some of them are getting equipment out of a couple of big vans blocking the way to the bike sheds and back gate; others are shouting orders.

Standing at the center of this mad, chaotic swirl of activity is a tall, slim man in a leather jacket, a huge cigar clamped in his mouth.

Billy sees a large camera being set up beside the man, realizes this must be — a movie crew! Billy is intrigued, thinks it's so cool, wonders why they're here, assumes they must be using the school as a location. It's odd he hasn't heard anything about it, he thinks. Then he shrugs, decides it's probably being kept quiet to make sure hordes of gawking kids don't hang around.

After all, it isn't every day you get to watch a movie crew in action, maybe catch a glimpse of a star or two. That's what Billy wants to do, anyway. He doesn't think anyone has noticed him and quickly slips into the shadows beneath the fire escape, excited now, determined to see as much as he can. At least it might help him forget his troubles, forget Mickey for a while.

Things gradually settle down as Billy watches, the chaos resolving itself into ordered bustle, then calm, the crew in position. The tall man still stands at the center of it all, a young woman with a clipboard beside him. The man whispers something to her, and she marches off, heading toward the two vans — and Billy suddenly realizes the tall man must be the movie director.

An expectant hush falls, everyone seemingly waiting, the only sounds a soft swish of wind, a discarded candy wrapper scuffling over the pavement.

Then a strange, dark figure emerges from one of the vans, a man wearing a top hat and a flowing black cape with a red satin lining. Billy can see he is in makeup, his face a mask of what's supposed to be scarred and burnt flesh. The man is holding a knife, its slender blade flashing under the lights.

Billy knows that the man is an actor, but it's still a spooky sight.

The actor makes his way through the crew, stops in front of them, stands motionless like a wax dummy, the knife by his side. Billy wonders if he's a star, but it could be anybody under that makeup. Billy realizes one thing, at least: It must be a horror movie they're shooting here today.

Soon the Clipboard Lady, for that's the name Billy gives her, emerges from the same van, looking rather anxious, hurries back to the director.

"I'm afraid we might have something of a problem," she says. "It seems that no one's actually remembered to book an extra for this scene."

"What do you mean, no one remembered?" snarls the director, turning to glare at her, the cigar moving up and down in the corner of his mouth as he speaks. "Those incompetent casting people should have taken care of that!" he continues. "Now listen, I want you to get on the phone immediately —"

"I've spoken to them already," the Clipboard Lady replies. "They don't know why it wasn't done, and they can't get an extra on such short notice."

"I don't believe this!" exclaims the director. He takes the cigar from his mouth, drops it to the ground, grinds it under his heel. Billy is fascinated, watches the director's every move. "So what am I supposed to do now? The crew's on overtime, I've got a deadline to meet. . . ." He paces up and down, stops, glares at the Clipboard Lady again. "Well, I'm not going to waste a whole night's shooting. We'll have to find an extra ourselves."

"But I don't see how or where," says the Clipboard Lady.

Billy notices that most of the crew are no longer paying any attention. Some are reading newspapers, others chatting quietly, and the spooky actor is doing nothing. In fact, he doesn't appear to have moved a single muscle.

Then Billy hears something that almost makes him stop breathing.

"Well, what about . . . him?" says the director, and points at Billy.

Billy feels time itself stretching, the

director's gesture somehow slipping into slow motion, his voice deepening, that last word *him* lengthening, as if it's being pulled from his mouth, his gaze fixed on Billy across the distance between them. And all the others turn now to stare at Billy, their heads moving in unison, their eyes boring into him. . . .

BONY FINGERS

Billy panics, retreats farther into the shadows, soon finds his back against the wall. He thinks about making a dash for the main gates, but it's too late.

The director is advancing on him, the Clipboard Lady in his wake.

Time reverts to its normal speed. Or does it? The director moves quickly, jerkily almost, his progress marked by sudden leaps during which he appears to cover a lot of ground, like a character in one of those old silent movies. Billy shakes his head, thinks that maybe it's a trick of the lights.

"Hi there!" says the director, stopping a couple of yards in front of Billy, at the edge of the fire escape's shadow. He's smiling, but Billy doesn't find that particularly reassuring. "Now, don't be frightened, I don't bite," the director continues. "Well, not very often, anyway," he adds, and laughs softly. "So, how would you like to be in the movies, kid?"

"Who, me?" says Billy, his voice

embarrassingly squeaky. He can feel himself blushing. "I wouldn't," he murmurs. "Thanks all the same."

"Come on," says the director. "I'd have thought most kids your age would jump at the chance. Besides, you'll be doing me a real favor."

"Well . . ." says Billy, and realizes the director has edged closer.

"Great!" the man says, and reaches out to grab Billy's arm.

The power of his grip is disconcerting, his long, bony fingers sinking into the flesh of Billy's right bicep. For an instant, Billy hangs back, resisting the pull. Then he gives in, not wanting to cause trouble.

The director drags Billy off, doesn't let go till they're standing in front of the crew. Billy has to shield his eyes from the bright lights with his hand.

"I'm not sure about this," the Clipboard Lady tells the director.

She's whispering, but Billy can hear her every word. She must have followed them over, Billy thinks, although he hadn't noticed her.

"Quite apart from the insurance implications," she says, "he's obviously got no experience. . . ."

"So what?" the director snaps. "If you ask me, any fool can see he's absolutely perfect for the job. He certainly won't have to do any acting. . . ."

Billy stands there listening as the two of them argue, the crew reverting to its previous state of boredom and inactivity.

Billy isn't sure how to take what the director has just said, but what worries him more is that the Clipboard Lady might manage to talk the director out of using him.

For Billy has changed his mind. He has decided that being in the movies might be a terrific idea, a great opportunity to do something that's way past cool. Billy can imagine the look on Mickey's face when his tormentor discovers that he's in a movie. What better way to show Mickey that he isn't a loser?

"Er . . . excuse me?" Billy says, interrupting the argument. The director and the Clipboard Lady stop talking, turn to look at him. "I'd really like to do it."

"Ah, that's the spirit," says the director,

and grins at him. The Clipboard Lady sighs and rolls her eyes, but the director ignores her. He puts his arm around Billy, leads him away quickly, Billy feeling as if his feet barely touch the ground, till the director suddenly stops by one of the vans. "So, you'll probably want to know what you're letting yourself in for, right, kid?"

"Yes, I would," says Billy, trying to sound positive and look intelligent, telling himself to go along with what the director wants, not to spoil things.

"Well, making a movie is kind of like making a cake," says the director, producing another large cigar and lighting it with lots of puffing. The smoke is thick

and white and pungent, a cloud that soon envelops them both. It catches Billy in the back of the throat and he smothers a cough. "So what you need first, of course," the director says, "is a good recipe. A script . . ."

Suddenly under the director's arm, Billy sees a wedge of paper bound in a red cover, held together by silver brads. *That's very strange,* Billy thinks. He doesn't remember seeing the director holding it before. But he decides that the director must have had it with him all along and he just hadn't noticed. Things don't just materialize out of thin air. . . . Billy frowns

at the thought, concentrates on the director's voice.

"In a way, the script gives me a list of the ingredients that go into the film," the director is saying, "and instructions on how to put them together. I also need a few tools, some utensils." He pauses, takes the cigar from his mouth, and vaguely gestures at the crew with it. "But I'm the one in charge. I'm the head chef, as it were; I tell everybody what to do. But even more important, I'm the one who has 'final cut.' Know what that is, kid?"

"I'm not really sure." Billy's mind is filled with an image of the director cutting a cake with a knife — like the one the scary-looking actor is carrying — although he knows that can't be right. From the corner of an eye, Billy glimpses some of the crew smirking. But when he glances around, there are no smirks — just blank, expressionless faces staring at him. Billy shivers.

"It means I'm the one who gets to decide what the cake ultimately looks like," the director is saying. Billy quickly turns his gaze back to him. "Once we've done all the actual shooting, I do the editing, I decide which pieces of film go where, what gets put in, what gets left out. Control, kid, that's what matters. Who's in control of the final product. OK, is that all clear?"

"Yeah, absolutely," says Billy, although the truth is that he's confused and starting to feel out of his depth. "Recipe, script, ingredients, final cut . . ."

"And you're an ingredient," the director declares, "a pinch of something essential." The director looks beyond Billy. The Clipboard Lady frowns at him, taps her watch. "I know, the clock is ticking," the director mutters. "Come on," he says to Billy. "It's time I did some cooking."

The director rams his cigar back in his mouth and strides off.

Billy trots after him, and once again something very strange seems to happen to time. Billy feels he's hardly taken two steps when suddenly, he's standing beside the spooky-looking actor — who Billy thought was at least fifty feet away. Now that he's closer to him, Billy can see that the actor's makeup is amazing, the supposed scars and burnt flesh scarily, eye-poppingly real.

Billy feels a little queasy, realizes the director is talking again.

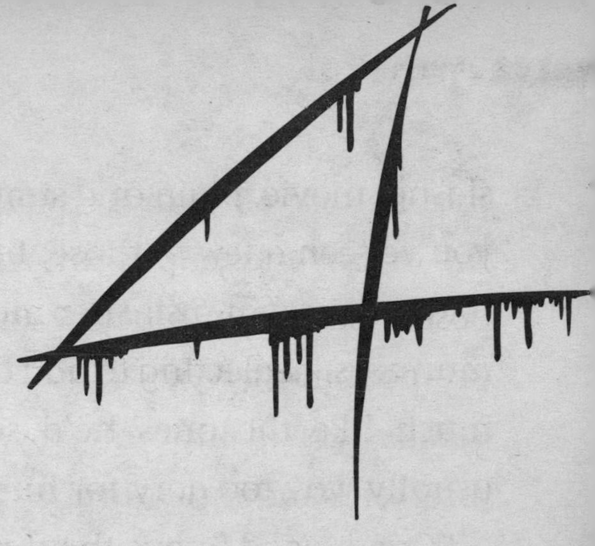

SLASHER MOVIE

"Let's get down to business," the director says. The crew pays attention. Newspapers are folded; conversations come to an end.

"You don't need to know the storyline in detail, Billy," says the director. "It's a slasher movie, plain and simple, and I bet you've seen a few of those, haven't you?"

"I know what a slasher movie is," Billy murmurs, neglecting to add that he didn't much like the ones he'd seen. They're usually way too gory for him.

"Good, good," says the director. "Well, in this scene, the villain, as played by our friend here, chases you, the victim." Billy stiffens a little when he hears that. "You enter running from the left" — the director continues, making a square with his index fingers and thumbs, looking through it as if it's a camera viewfinder — "and you keep running while we pan. Then you exit from the right, over there." Billy glances in the direction the director is pointing, sees he means near the fire escape. "Got that?" the director asks.

"I think so," says Billy, nervous now at what he's being asked to do, his uneasiness focusing on that word *victim*. "But that's like acting, isn't it?" says Billy. "And you said I wasn't going to do any. I thought an extra just sort of stood in the background. . . ."

"I hope you're not going to let me down," the director snaps, treating Billy to the same glare he'd given the Clipboard Lady. "I mean, it's not exactly rocket science, is it? All you've got to do is run, oh, and maybe look scared witless at the same time. You can do that, Billy, can't you?"

Billy is taken aback by the sudden sharpness in the director's voice, the anger and sarcasm, the abrupt change from the friendliness of a moment ago. He feels a small stirring of anger in himself, a sense that he doesn't want to be talked to in this way, that he doesn't want to be in a movie as a victim. It might even be the wrong message to send to Mickey Travis.

Then again, whatever the role, it would still be impressive for him just to be in a movie, wouldn't it? Besides, Billy doesn't like thinking how the director might react if he pulls out now. He has a feeling the director might give him a seriously hard time. So Billy decides to play along. He takes a deep breath, pushes down his anger, swallows his resentment.

"Yeah, I can do that," he says. Then something slightly puzzling occurs to him. “Hey, how do you know my name? I don’t think I mentioned it.”

“You must have,” says the director, all smiles, quickly turning to the crew before Billy can disagree with him. “Places, everybody. Billy, your mark is on the right, over there,” the director adds, pointing with his cigar to a small white cross chalked on the pavement right beside the scary actor.

The director returns to his position

beside the camera, where a folding canvas chair has suddenly appeared. He sits down in it, holds the script on his lap. The Clipboard Lady is standing next to him, her face blank.

Billy does what he's told, walks over to his mark. He feels more confused than ever. He's sure he didn't tell the director his name, and now there are a few other things he's beginning to find strange in this whole setup. For instance, Billy has noticed that no one else seems to be feeling the cold like him. Some of the crew are even wearing Hawaiian shirts with short sleeves.

"Silence on set!" the Clipboard Lady yells, her voice loud and piercing.

Billy sees a crew member appear in

front of him, a man holding up a clapper board. "Scene sixty-six, take one!" the man calls out, slamming down the top strip of the clapper board with a *CRACK!* like a gunshot.

"Action!" the director says. Billy looks around — and his blood freezes.

The scary-looking actor isn't motionless anymore. In fact, the change in him from stillness to threatening movement happens so fast it's terrifying. He leans forward, ready to spring, the knife raised, its point glinting under the lights, a convincing expression of hate on that hideous face. His cape briefly billows out behind him, flickering red and black.

Then he leaps, and Billy runs, desperate

to keep as much distance as possible between himself and that knife. But it's only a movie, Billy thinks, part of his mind registering the crew as he races past them. Yet the sound of pounding feet on

the pavement behind him is real enough. Billy wants to look over his shoulder but doesn't dare. He wonders how close the actor is, how close the blade is to the flesh of his back, his soft, vulnerable back. . . .

"CUT!" a voice yells just as Billy reaches the shadows beneath the fire escape. Billy skids to a halt, worried by the word for a second, then realizes it's the director telling the cameraman to stop filming. Billy looks around, his breath rasping, his heart thudding, sees the actor close behind him. The actor slowly lowers the knife, stares at Billy for a second . . . and hisses. Then he turns,

sweeps his cape around him, and stalks away, back to his mark.

Billy uneasily watches him go, feels there is something very unpleasant about him. He's never been hissed at before, not even by Mickey Travis and his thugs.

Suddenly, Billy feels the director standing close beside him.

"Don't worry about your costar, Billy," says the director. "He's just one of those actors who really likes to get into a part, you know what I mean?"

Billy doesn't know, and he's not sure he cares anymore, either. And why is the director referring to the actor as his costar? Billy's not a star in the movie — he's just an extra, isn't he? *This is all too much,*

Billy thinks, the strangeness, the scariness of the take, the crew staring at him. . . .

"Can I go home now?" says Billy. "That was OK, wasn't it?"

"Well, OK is about right, Billy," the director says. "But I'm pretty sure we can do a hell of a lot better. I want to try another take, only this time —"

"I'm sorry," Billy mutters. "I'd really like to help you, but I —"

"Oh, no, I haven't finished with you yet, Billy," snarls the director, his voice deepening again to a rumble that makes Billy's head throb. The director is scowling, his eyes seeming to flash red at Billy for the briefest instant. "Not by a long shot," he says. "You'll do exactly what I tell you."

BLOODSTAIN

Billy is scowling himself now. He's angry with the director, doesn't like the way he's being treated. He feels like walking around the vans and out the back gate, forgetting the whole thing. But he sighs, decides to take the path of least resistance, go along with what the director wants from him.

"OK, then," says Billy, and shrugs. He slowly walks back to his mark, taking his place beside the spooky actor. He'll just do this one last thing for them, Billy thinks, and then they'll leave him alone. They're bound to.

A happy smile spreads slowly over the director's face, and Billy notices that the entire crew is definitely smirking at him now. Billy feels more uneasy than ever. What he hears next doesn't make him feel any better.

"Well done, Billy," says the director. "You've passed the test."

"Test?" says Billy. "What test? I didn't know I'd been taking one."

“Well, you have, Billy,” says the director, his cigar bobbing up and down as he speaks. “You’ve proved you can play the role of a victim. Perfectly.”

“Hey, just hold on a second,” Billy mutters, his anger flooding back.

“Silence on set!” yells the Clipboard Lady. The clapper board man leaps in front of Billy, grins crazily at him, holds his clapper board up very close to Billy’s face. “Scene sixty-six — take two!” the man shouts, almost screaming it out, then slams the top section down again and leaps aside.

“Once more, with feeling,” roars the director. “OK, Billy — action!”

And suddenly, the spooky actor is moving again. But he doesn’t crouch first as he did before, ready to spring — he simply leaps forward, slashing at Billy with the knife. Billy turns and runs, and something happens to time again. Billy feels himself moving slowly, almost as if the air around him has become thick and liquid and resists the motion of his arms and legs.

Billy looks around, and wishes he hadn't. The actor is close behind him, the knife

raised, its blade flashing. Billy tears his eyes away, feels a surge of panic, his breath rasping, his heart leaping. The shadows beneath the fire escape are just ahead of him. He has to make it, he's nearly there, three more paces, two more, one more — and then Billy feels a blow to his upper arm.

"CUT!" the director yells, his voice drawn out, a long, slow groan making that one small word resonate and echo inside Billy's skull.

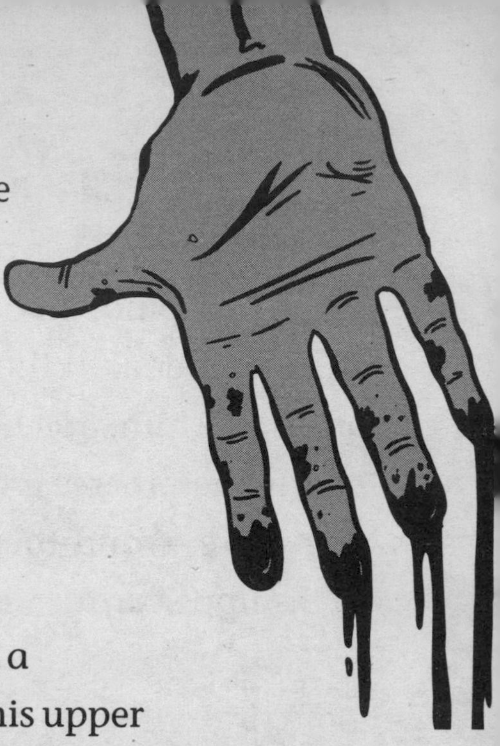

Billy arrives at the fire escape, skids to a halt, gingerly touches the place where he'd felt the blow, a spot on the back of his upper arm. His jacket there is slashed and, as he explores the torn material, Billy feels a wetness on his fingertips and simultaneously a sharp pain. Time jolts back into normal speed. He peers at his fingertips, sees a dark stain on them.

He realizes it must be blood. His blood. The actor has cut him. . . .

Billy stares at the blood for a moment.

There's quite a lot of it, although he doesn't think he's been hurt badly. But he shouldn't have been hurt at all, should he? This is a movie, and however scary that actor might look, he's still only an actor, isn't he? So what is going on? It has to be a mistake, Billy decides; the stupid man has simply gotten into his part way too much.

Billy is facing the wall and suddenly, the back of his neck starts prickling the way it does when you have the feeling that you're being stared at. It's strangely quiet behind him, too, the only sound the wind whistling softly over the pavement. Billy is almost too scared to turn around, but he does, and once again this afternoon, his mouth drops open — with sheer terror this time.

The world seems to shift beneath his feet and he feels sick. For the director, the Clipboard Lady, the entire movie crew, all of them have been transformed into creatures from the most terrifying horror movie — the most terrifying nightmare — imaginable. Only the scary actor remains the same, and Billy realizes that's because he's not an actor, and he's not made up. The hideous scars, the burnt flesh, the glinting knife . . . everything is real. But the scary actor's face is nothing compared to those of the monster crew. Billy closes his eyes, tells himself he must be dreaming, that none of this is happening.

"Oh, but I'm afraid it is, Billy," he hears the director say.

Billy wonders if he'd spoken his thoughts aloud, then realizes he hadn't. He takes a deep breath of cold air, counts to three, opens his eyes. If anything, the scene before him is worse, even more frightening — some of the crew levitating above the lights, cackling as they swoop through the air, a couple of them diving at him, and up and away again. Billy can feel his heart beating as if it's about to explode, his whole body trembling.

There's no denying the evidence of his senses. And deep down, he knows that from the moment he'd walked into this part of the playground he'd felt something wasn't right. But he'd let himself be fooled, hadn't he? Although he can't worry about that now, he tells himself. He needs to find a way out of this. Billy glances around, searching for an escape route, his eyes darting. . . .

"Forget it, Billy," says the director. "You're not going anywhere."

ALL ETERNITY

Billy sees that he's surrounded. He retreats into the shadows beneath the fire escape but soon finds his back to the wall again, feels the cut in his arm throbbing. Billy presses his shoulder blades against the bricks, wishes he could vanish through them. The creatures are advancing on him.

"Don't come any closer!" he shouts at last. "You won't get away with this. Someone will see what you're doing from the street. Help! HELP!"

"There's no point calling for help, Billy," says the director, laughing softly again, although he does hold up his hand, halting the crew behind him. They stand and stare at Billy, their eyes glowing red. "The street's a different world," the director continues, smiling horribly at him, "and nobody knows what's happening in here. Nobody but us. And you, of course."

"But what *is* happening?" Billy asks, trying his hardest to stay calm, to keep his voice steady. "I don't understand. Who are you? What are you?"

"So many questions, Billy," says the director. "Let's just say that we're not the people you thought we were, although I think we gave an excellent performance, don't you? But then we've had plenty of practice at this sort of thing. You could call us spirits. Or maybe *demons* is a better word."

The creatures smirk, and Billy feels his stomach tighten.

"OK, I believe you," he mutters. "But what do you want with me?"

"I've already told you," says the director. "I just want you to be in my movie, that's all. The script demands a victim — and you're so good at being one. That's the reason we were drawn to you in the first place."

"What are you talking about?" Billy's voice is small and quiet.

"It's just like your buddy Mickey said," the director murmurs, and his face

flickers, morphing into Mickey's face while he speaks, his voice into Mickey's voice. *"You're a born loser, pal. It's written all over you, and you'll never, ever change. . . ."* The director becomes his hideous self again, smiles at Billy. "Of course, I had to be sure," he says. "So I kept pushing you, bullying you into doing what I wanted you to do. And you passed the test."

Suddenly, Billy finds himself thinking about Mickey. And now he realizes with a shock that Mickey had been testing him, too, seeing how far he could push him. It all falls into place. Billy sees that he looks like a loser to Mickey for one very simple reason — he has always acted like one. Going along with whatever Mickey was doing, not causing any trouble, even hiding . . .

He should have drawn the line from the start, thinks Billy, whatever the consequences. Suddenly, Billy feels angry with himself for putting up with someone like Mickey Travis — for letting a lowlife like Mickey bully him. The anger swiftly replaces his fear, and he stops trembling.

"Well, I'm still not convinced he's right for the part," the Clipboard Lady is saying, her voice the same, her face a mask of horror. "I mean, he can't be very bright if he fell for all that awful stuff you came out with about making a movie being like making a cake. I don't know how I kept a straight face."

"I thought it was rather clever," the director snaps at her, several members of the crew snickering at him behind his back. "Anyway, he doesn't need to be bright, does he? As I said, he just needs to run and be scared witless, and he does that brilliantly. OK, that's enough chit-chat. Time for another take. . . ."

"Hold on," says Billy, his attention returning to what's happening around him. "You expect to let that creature chase me again, like he did before?"

"Oh, yes, Billy," says the director, grinning happily. "In fact, I expect you to let him chase you again and again and again, only he's going to catch you every time and do nasty, gory things to you. And when we get bored with that scenario, we'll think of something else equally terrifying. . . . You're going to become very familiar with the word *CUT*, and we're going to have so much fun watching you suffer . . . for all eternity. OK, places, everybody!"

And Billy instantly finds himself standing on his white cross once more.

The crew members cackle and rub their hands together as they do what they're told.

The scary actor takes up his position, raises his knife, gives Billy a chilling little wave, mimes a few slashing movements as though he's warming up. The director sits in his folding chair, the script on his lap, the Clipboard Lady beside him. Billy frowns, hates the way they sit there looking smug.

"Silence on the set!" the Clipboard Lady calls out. The creature with the clapper board capers madly in front of Billy. "Scene sixty-six, take three!" he yells.

But Billy pushes past him before he can slam the top of the clapper board down, before the director can say, "Action!" and start the nightmare rolling.

"NO!" Billy shouts at the top of his voice. "I WON'T DO IT!"

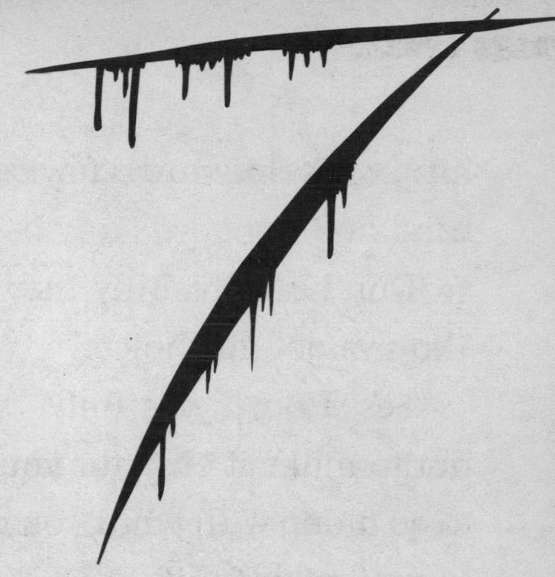

FINAL CUT

The crew's smiles vanish as Billy's words echo around them. Suddenly, the wind picks up, whistling through this small section of playground, ruffling clothes and hair. The director slowly rises from his chair, puts the script down on it behind him, walks forward a few paces. He stares hard at Billy.

"Don't be silly, Billy," says the director. "You've got no choice."

"Yes, I do," says Billy. "And I choose not to make it easy for you. I choose not to go along with what you want. I choose to spoil your fun!"

"Ah, but you're forgetting one thing, Billy," says the director. "It's all written in the script, and you'll never change it. You're my victim now."

"Is that right?" says Billy, his anger suddenly turning into a cold fury. The director's words have also given him an idea. Billy suddenly dashes forward, runs through the crew before any of them can grab him, dodges around the director, and finally reaches his chair.

Billy grabs the script, sits down in the chair with it on his lap.

The head of every creature there swivels in unison to stare at him, and a low wail issues from their throats. The sound blends with the wind's moan.

"Give it to me, Billy," the director says. "Give it to me now."

Billy looks at the director, notices that he seems, well . . . worried.

"I don't think I will," Billy replies, realizing that he's definitely on to something. "I want to see exactly what is written in this script of yours."

Billy opens it, flicks through, is amazed.

The script begins with a scene in the boys' room featuring characters named Billy Gibson and Mickey Travis and Tweedledum and Tweedledee. Then the character named Billy emerges from the school, sees a movie crew, talks to somebody called "the director." . . . It was all there, everything that had happened to him since he'd hidden in the boys' room. And there were more pages, more lines beyond the last ones he'd spoken, scenes that made Billy wince as his eyes skimmed over them.

But a line early in the script had caught Billy's eye, something about a red pen. Billy reaches into his pocket, pulls out the pen, stares at it for a moment. He hears another wail. He glances up at the faces watching him.

Now they're actually looking terrified, every one of them — the director, the Clipboard Lady, the actor with the knife, the whole creepy crew. *And so they should be,* thinks Billy. He smiles, leans back in the chair, taps the script with the pen. He's good at writing stories, isn't he? So why shouldn't he change this one, cross out what was coming, give it a different ending?

"I don't like this script," says Billy. The wail grows in volume and intensity. "I can't do much about what's already

happened. But I can certainly make sure I like what happens next, can't I?" He pulls off the pen cap, opens the script at the point they'd reached, draws a red line across the page, across the next one, and the next, finally ripping pages out, crumpling them up and throwing them down. But the last one is blank, and Billy holds on to it, smooths it out on the rest of the script. He thinks for a second.

Then he begins to write, saying the words as he scribbles them down.

"Billy sits in the director's chair and suddenly, the nightmare movie crew starts to fade, then vanish, one by one. The same happens to the vans and equipment and even the torn-out pages of script, to the scary actor, to the Clipboard Lady, until only the director is left. He stands motionless, a shrunken, pathetic figure, a boogeyman who isn't frightening anymore."

Billy stops writing, looks at the director one last time.

"I'd like to say it's been nice knowing you," says Billy. "But it hasn't."

Billy looks down and writes more, the words coming quickly now as he hurries to the end. "The director himself starts to fade. He shakes his fist at Billy, but it's

too late. The director vanishes with a faint *POP,* the air rushing in to fill the space he's been occupying, the burning red tip of his cigar the last part of him to disappear."

Billy sighs, stops writing, folds up the piece of paper, and puts it in his jacket pocket along with the pen.

Billy stands, the chair vanishes, the air shimmering around him for a moment. The wind whistles softly over the empty pavement, and he raises his head, looks up at the sky. It's free of clouds. A few lonely stars glitter above the school, the

playground, the back gate. *Time to go home,* thinks Billy. He walks away, notices that his arm isn't throbbing anymore, that his sleeve isn't slashed. He pauses, wonders briefly if it had all happened.

Then Billy realizes he's still holding the script, the part he didn't rip out and throw away. So there's no doubting it. He walks on, stops by the back gate. Beside

it is a small trash can. It's usually stuffed with candy wrappers and crushed soda cans, but tonight it's empty.

Billy looks at the wedge of paper — then rams it in the can. *Good riddance,* he thinks, and goes out through the gate, into the street. He's still got the pen, though, so he knows he can write another movie. A much better one, in which he tells his mom and dad and his teachers about Mickey, makes them believe him and do something. A movie in which he stands up to Mickey.

If he can deal with the director, he can deal with anybody.

Billy Gibson is the only person who's going to be in control of his movie in the future. He's the one who'll have the final cut. Billy turns the corner, stops, takes a deep breath, lets it out, feels the tension drain away. Billy smiles.

He is really, really looking forward to school tomorrow.

FIN
CU

TONY BRADMAN — WORDS

I WAS BORN IN LONDON IN 1954, AND WAS terrified at an early age by a lizard that fell out of a tree that I mistook for a deadly snake, my grandmother who took snuff and threatened me with a cane when I was naughty, and possible gory death when I ran through the window of a Laundromat, shattering the glass into tiny pieces with my head. These days I try to avoid things like that, and get most of my frights from watching scary movies and reading scary books. Or writing them.

I still live in London, a dark and ancient city, full of odd corners where nasty things have happened, and where I sometimes worry about bumping into my grandmother's ghost. It hasn't happened yet, but if it does, I just might turn the experience into another Tale of Terror. I hope reading this one scares you as much as writing it terrified me. . . .

MARTIN CHATTERTON — PICTURES

IT WAS ALL GOING SO WELL UNTIL BRADMAN came along. . . . An idyllic upbringing in Liverpool. College. Marriage to a devoted wife. Two lovely children. A faithful dog. Twenty years spent quietly illustrating, designing, and writing all over the world. I had a good life. A secure, unremarkable, safe existence. And then . . . then . . . Bradman made me work on Tales of Terror and everything changed.

I haven't slept in weeks. I don't dare — the nightmares will come back. The voices keep asking me to come out, but I won't. Not yet. They can't make me. I'm safe in here. Safe with the lights on and the door locked and bolted . . .

Let me give you a word of advice. Come closer. I don't want them to hear. Right up to the crack in the door. I'll whisper it. "Don't read this book!"